To Charlotte,
Love from,

....

"Sweet little Charlotte,
time to shut your eyes.
The moon has come out,
there are stars in the skies."

"But I'm not very tired;
I don't want to count sheep.
I wonder how all of my friends
get to sleep?"

"That's a good question.
Well, why don't we see?
Hold my hand tightly, Charlotte,
stay close to me."

"Here are the ducklings wading out of the lake. They're all nice and clean and now barely awake!"

"Deer share happy thoughts.
It makes them all smile.
They'll settle down
then be asleep
in a while."

"These hedgehogs are S-T-R-E-T-C-H-I-N-G!
It's the start of their day.
At bedtime they'll end it
the very same way!"

"Do you hear lullabies
as the baby birds sing?
Soon they'll be dreaming
beneath Mom's soft wing."

"The squirrels like stories
at bedtime, it seems.
I'll bet it's a tale that will
give them sweet dreams."

Now Charlotte is sleepy.
The moon's in the sky.
"Please can I have
a good night lullaby?"

"Sweet little Charlotte,
I hope you sleep tight.
May you dream the most
beautiful dreams.
Night night..."

Charlotte's Countdown to Bedtime

10 Put away your toys

9 Take a bath

8 Brush your teeth

7 Use the bathroom

6 Wash your hands

5
Change
into your
pajamas

4
Share a story
about your day

3
Switch off the
big light and get
into bed

2
Read your
favorite storybook,
*Night Night
Charlotte*

1
Say "Night night"
and drift off
to sleep

z
z
z

Written by J.D. Green
Illustrated by Joanne Partis
Designed by Ryan Dunn

Copyright © Hometown World Ltd. 2019

Put Me In The Story is a
registered trademark of Sourcebooks, Inc.
All rights reserved.

Published by Put Me In The Story,
a publication of Sourcebooks, Inc.
P.O. Box 4410, Naperville, Illinois 60567-4410
(630) 536-1104
www.putmeinthestory.com

Date of Production: October 2019
Run Number: 5015993
Printed and bound in Italy (LG)
10 9 8 7 6 5 4 3 2 1

FSC
www.fsc.org

MIX
Paper from
responsible sources
FSC® C023419

put **me** in the **story**®

Bestselling books starring your child!
www.putmeinthestory.com